WHAT A MASTERPIECE!

RICCARDO GUASCO

EERDMANS BOOKS FOR YOUNG READERS
GRAND RAPIDS, MICHIGAN

DISCOVER THE ART

In this book you have met artwork from many different centuries. Some masterpieces might be familiar to you, and others you might be seeing for the first time!

1
Pablo Picasso
Joie de Vivre, 1946

8
Salvador Dalí
The Persistence of Memory, 1931

2
Mario Sironi
Urban Landscape, 1922

9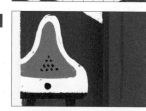
Piet Mondrian
Composition with Red, Yellow, and Blue, 1937–42

3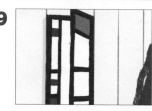
Paul Klee
Urban Composition with Yellow Windows, 1919

10
Alberto Giacometti
Walking Man I, 1960

4
Vincent van Gogh
The Starry Night, 1889

11
Marcel Duchamp
Fountain, 1917

5
Vincent van Gogh
Self-Portrait with Bandaged Ear, 1889

12
M. C. Escher
Relativity, 1953

6
Édouard Manet
The Luncheon on the Grass, 1863

13
Giorgio Morandi
Still Life, 1952

7
Vincent van Gogh
The Bedroom in Arles, 1888

14
Amedeo Modigliani
Jeanne Hébuterne in Red Shawl, 1917

W hat a Masterpiece! was originally published in Italy for the Festival of Creative Culture, which celebrated Europe's strong cultural heritage and its potential for future creativity. Driven by our imagination and our desire to express ourselves, humans have created countless masterpieces over the centuries. These works of art can help build bridges that unite people across generations and cultures.

This wordless book draws the reader into the story through bold colors and strong, often familiar images. The character wakes up and travels throughout his day, ultimately arriving at a great tree of art to which everyone can contribute. The story is an adventure in the imagination: every scene contains a suggestion, an invitation to discover another significant creator who has come before us. Gauguin, van Gogh, Modigliani, Klee—these and many others appear in this exuberant romp through art history that unites and invites us to contribute, together, to the creation of new masterpieces.

RICCARDO GUASCO is the illustrator of *A is for Donkeys*, which was self-published with Jonathan Hope. His favorite artists include Pablo Picasso and Lyonel Feininger. Riccardo's work has appeared in *The New Yorker* and *Los Angeles Magazine*, and he is also the co-founder of the Inchiostro Festival, a gathering of illustrators, calligraphers, and art printers. He lives in Alessandria, Italy.

Visit Riccardo's blog at riccardoguasco.tumblr.com or follow him on Instagram @guascoriccardo.